D0263220

ANIMAL
Adventure Club

For Lizzie, Anna and Andrew – M.S.
For Toby, with all my love – H.G.

Kelpies is an imprint of Floris Books
First published in 2019 by Floris Books

Endmatter illustrations by Floris Books

The publisher acknowledges subsidy from
Creative Scotland towards the publication
of this volume

Also available as an eBook

British Library CIP data available
ISBN 978-178250-556-3
Printed & bound by MBM Print SCS Ltd, Glasgow

The Baby Deer Rescue

Written by
Michelle Sloan

Illustrated by
Hannah George

Dooey Burn
Bridge
faerie
circle
Play
park
Craggy
Woods
West
Hide
Loch Dooey
East
Hide
mountain bike
track
The Folly
Mungo's
Island
Roman Fort
boat sheds
Drookit
Dell
cycle path
Boggy Burn

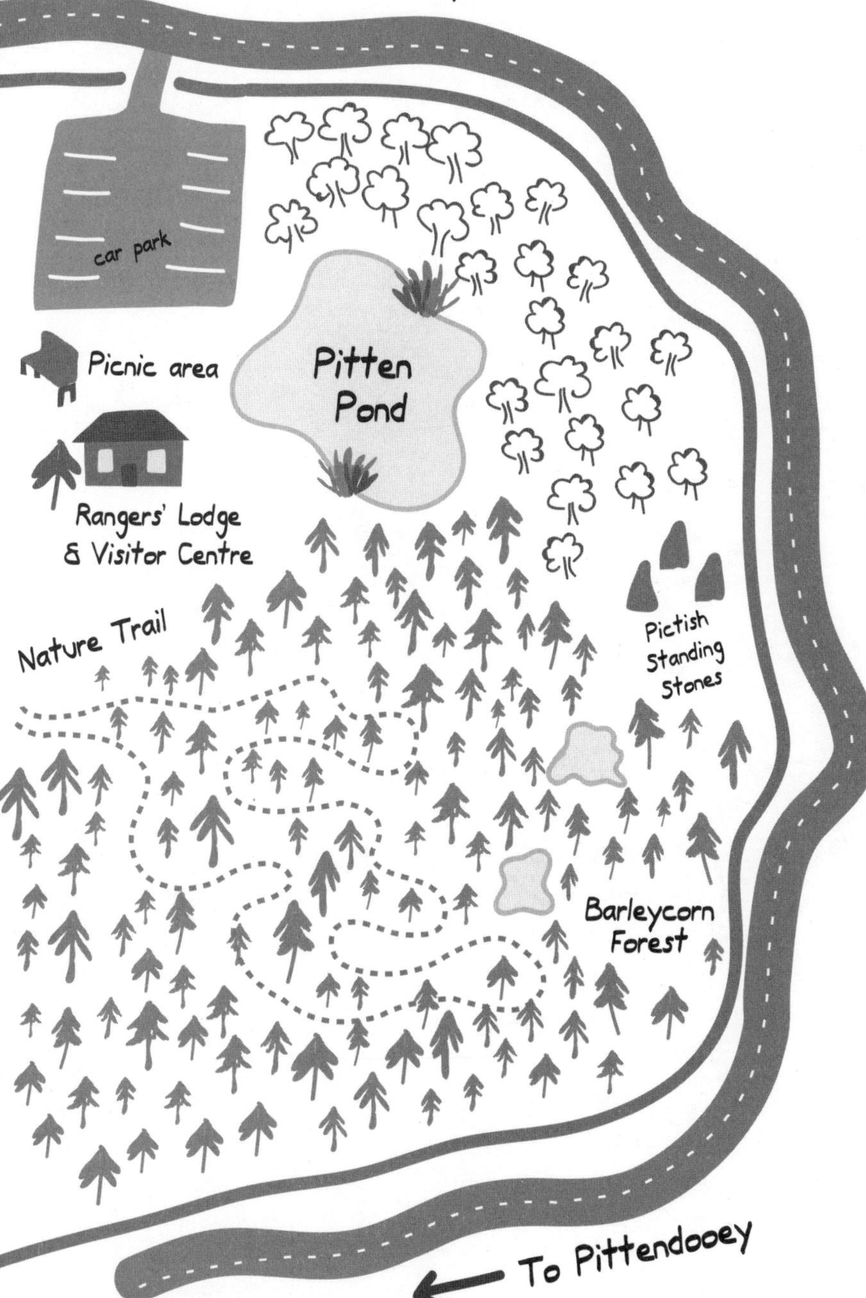
Entrance to Pittendooey Nature Reserve
car park
Picnic area
Pitten Pond
Rangers' Lodge & Visitor Centre
Nature Trail
Pictish Standing Stones
Barleycorn Forest
To Pittendooey

1

Isla MacLeod drummed her feet on the floor of the Pittendooey Nature Reserve rangers' lodge. It was nearly four o'clock: time for the Animal Adventure Club meeting. Three afternoons a week, Isla and her friends Buzz and Gracie came to the nature reserve after school to help the rangers and, best of all, look after animals! Buzz was here, but there was no sign of Gracie. Isla couldn't wait for her to arrive so they could go out on patrol.

"Can you give me a hand with Spiky?" called Buzz. He was helping Lisa, the head ranger, to take care of a poorly hedgehog.

"Lisa asked me to give him his ear drops."

"Sure," said Isla. "We can help Spiky while we wait for Gracie." Isla jumped up and headed towards Buzz and Spiky at the far end of the room. "Oof!" she said, pinching her nose. "Spiky's a bit smelly. Maybe we should have called him Stinky."

"That's why we keep him back here!" Buzz laughed, and opened Spiky's cage. There was a big pile of straw bundled in one corner. Isla put on a pair of thick gloves, then reached in and gently teased the straw away to reveal a large ball of sharp prickles.

"Hello, wee pal," said Isla softly, lifting the hedgehog out and placing him on a towel on the table. His prickles bristled.

"Try stroking his back," said Buzz. "That should relax him."

Sure enough, as Isla stroked him, the ball began to slowly unfurl. A tiny snuffly nose poked out, followed by a paw. Buzz leaned in and had a good look at the little hedgehog's face.

"He's looking much brighter," he said. Spiky let out a small squeak.

"Cheeky thing," said Buzz. He pulled a little bottle out of his pocket and tipped the drops into Spiky's tiny ears.

"I don't know how you manage to find his ears under all those prickles!" laughed Isla. "You're going to be a brilliant vet one day."

Buzz's face went red, but he smiled. "So, what's the Animal Adventure Club doing this afternoon?" he asked.

"Never mind this afternoon – we've got enough jobs to last us a month!" said Isla. She grabbed her notebook out of her rucksack and read aloud:

1. Help Lisa find good trees for hanging bat boxes, then mark them with chalk so we can find them later.

2. Collect bark, leaves, twigs, moss and pine cones for building bug hotels.
3. Make fact sheets to teach visitors about the animals in the reserve.

"Whew!" said Buzz. "Sounds like hard work. Remember we've got to fill the bird feeders too. Speaking of feeding, I'm getting hungry and we haven't even started yet! Do you think we can fit in a biscuit or two before we go?"

But Isla didn't have time to answer, because a familiar voice outside shouted, "Buzz! Isla! Where are you?"

"We're in the lodge," Isla called back.

The door burst open. "Have you seen Lisa?" gasped a sweaty Gracie.

"She's fixing some fencing by the boat sheds," said Buzz, carefully placing Spiky back in his cage. "What's up?"

"There's no time to go and get her then," said Gracie. "There's an animal up by Craggy Woods in real danger! Bring Lisa's cutters, Isla."

Isla put them in her rucksack and they set off after Gracie, who led the way around Loch Dooey at a cracking pace. Squabbling black-headed gulls shrieked and swooped overhead. Even though Isla was in a hurry, she noticed some tiny and very fluffy chicks bobbing on the water near the gulls' nesting area on the loch. She tried not to get distracted.

"What kind of animal is it?" asked Isla.

"I think it's a baby deer," puffed Gracie.

"You mean a fawn," corrected Buzz.

"Fine, a fawn," Gracie said impatiently. "I didn't have time to look properly. I was coming here on my bike when I heard screeches from the woods near the cycle path. I headed straight to the lodge to tell Lisa."

They bolted round the loch, over Dooey Burn Bridge and into Dritchel Woods. Gracie was a brilliant tracker and knew exactly which of the winding paths to take.

"Where now?" asked Isla.

"By the fence at the edge of the woods," said Gracie. They could hear distant cries.

Isla slowed down as they drew closer, and signalled to the others to be quiet. Gracie pointed to the far end of the fence. There, almost hidden in the long grass, was a tiny golden fawn. Its head was caught in the wires and it was crying pitifully.

"Look, it's bleeding," said Gracie. "Poor thing."

"We need to stay quiet so we don't frighten it any more," whispered Buzz. "Fawns can be scared of people."

The fawn was panicking and struggling because its head was stuck.

"We have to free it," Isla said quietly, "before it really hurts itself."

"But how?" asked Gracie, her eyes wide.

Isla took off her rucksack and crept closer. She knelt beside the fawn, wondering what to do. *Just stay still,* she told herself. *Maybe if I stay calm, the fawn will calm down too.*

After what seemed like a long time, something extraordinary happened: the fawn stopped wailing and thrashing, and its breathing became steadier, almost in time with Isla's.

"Pass me my rucksack please," whispered Isla.

Carefully, Gracie handed it to her, trying not to make a sound.

Still moving slowly and calmly, Isla took out a pair of gloves and a small pair of cutters. Checking it was safe and that the fawn was calm, she made one swift snip in the wire fence.

Instantly, the baby deer pulled out its head. For a split second, the animal stared at Isla with its huge dark-brown eyes and blinked with long, feathery eyelashes. Its shiny black nose twitched, and then it turned and bounded into the depths of the forest.

"Wowza!" said Buzz.

"Double wowza!" said Gracie.

Isla watched after the beautiful baby animal, glad it was free.

"It was bleeding, wasn't it?" said Gracie.

"I don't think there was much blood," added Buzz. "It should be fine."

Gracie nodded. "I hope so." She turned to Isla and helped her friend up. "Well done, Isla. You were so calm."

Isla shrugged and smiled. "Thanks Gracie. It's just as well you got to the lodge so fast. Any longer and the fawn might have been badly injured."

"C'mon," said Buzz. "Let's get back and tell Lisa all about it. And we've still got to go through all the Animal Adventure Club tasks you have on your list, Isla."

"And eat some biscuits, I bet?" she said cheekily, nudging Buzz.

"Too right!" he said. "There's a packet of custard creams waiting for us, and I'm *starving*! Let's go!"

2

"Isla, has your hair seen a brush today? It looks like pixies came in the night and tied it in knots!" called her mum.

Isla shook her bushy head and rolled her eyes.

"C'mon," said her mum. "You can brush it on the way to school, or we'll be late."

Isla grabbed a slice of toast with one hand and her schoolbag with the other, and jumped into the car. The village of Pittendooey was nestled between mountains in the Scottish Highlands. The nearest big town, Strathdooey, was a half-hour drive away. That's where Isla's mum worked as a nurse in the big health centre. Isla's dad lived in Strathdooey too and she spent every second weekend with him.

"Mum, is it OK if I put some food out in the garden?" Isla asked cautiously.

"What is it for this time? Or *who* is it for?" Isla's mum asked.

"Sorry, I thought I'd mentioned it," said Isla, nibbling her toast. "There's a fox in the garden. I saw paw prints, so I waited and spotted a fox and her cub."

Isla's mum sighed. "I'm not sure," she said. "I wouldn't know what to feed them." She glanced over at Isla. "And stop biting your nails," she added.

Isla sat on her fingers. "Foxes eat dog food," she said. "I've looked it up already."

"But is it safe to leave food for foxes, Isla?"

"It has a cub to feed, Mum! And it's really cute. Look, I've drawn a picture of it." She rummaged around in her bag for her journal. "Well, I tried to. I'm not very good at drawing."

"Oh, Isla," her mum said as they pulled up to the school gate. "It's just *more* animals to feed. You've already got your pet mice, and the bird feeders, and the bug hotel by the shed!"

"Mum, the bug hotel is hardly 'feeding animals'," said Isla, folding her arms tightly.

"Let's talk about it later," said her mum. "I'll pick you up from the reserve this evening."

"OK," said Isla, trying to keep her voice bright. She planted a buttery kiss on her mum's cheek and clambered out of the car.

"TGIF!" shouted her mum.

Isla looked blank.

"Thank goodnesss it's Friday!" laughed her mum. "Get it?"

Isla's face broke into a beaming smile. "TGIF!" she shouted back. She gave her mum a cheery wave and ambled across the playground towards the P6 lines.

"Hey Isla!" shouted a voice behind her. It was Buzz, running up and munching an apple. "Your stuff's about to fall out of your bag," he said, reaching to pull up the zip.

"Oops," said Isla. "Could you grab my journal actually? I want to show you something."

Buzz handed it to her and she flicked it open to the picture she'd drawn of the fawn.

"Hi guys!" Gracie ran up to them and peered at Isla's journal. "Nice picture, Isla," she said. "You're not as bad at drawing as you make out, you know." She looked Isla in the eye. "And you shouldn't be shy about your *other* talent either."

"Other talent? What do you mean?" asked Isla.

"You know, for calming animals, like you did with the fawn yesterday."

Isla blushed a little.

"You're an animal whisperer, Isla," said Buzz, his eyes wide.

The two girls looked at each other for a second before they burst out laughing.

"She doesn't have magic powers, Buzz!" snorted Gracie.

Isla giggled. "I just decided that it was best to keep still and quiet. Anyone could do it."

"Well, it *really* worked," said Buzz. "And I'm not sure just *anyone* could do it."

Isla stopped laughing and smiled. "Thanks, Buzz."

"I wonder how the baby deer is doing now?" asked Buzz.

"You mean fawn," corrected Gracie with a cheeky grin and Buzz laughed.

"Lisa said she'd look out for it, but maybe we should go back through Craggy Woods again this afternoon," said Isla, flicking through her journal. "We can have a look around and double check the fawn isn't lying injured somewhere."

"I'm in," said Gracie.

"Me too," added Buzz, and they all leaned in for an Animal Adventure Club fist bump.

"Is that a picture of a rabbit?" said a loud voice behind them. "Not bad, Isla. I like drawing as well, you know. I'll let you see some of mine sometime."

They all swung round to see new girl Lexi Budge. She had only been at the school for a few weeks but was already sticking her nose into everybody's business.

"It's a fawn, actually," said Isla quietly.

"Is it?" Lexi laughed. "Try making its legs longer. It looks a bit stumpy."

"Well, I think it's brilliant," said Gracie, folding her arms.

"Were you talking about going up to the reserve?" Lexi rambled on. "I go there *all* the time. My aunt Lisa is a ranger and she knows absolutely *everything* there is to know about

animals. So do I actually," she added, sticking her nose in the air.

"We know Lisa too, Lexi," Gracie said.

"Oh yeah, your wee club!" Lexi said. "What's it called again? The Fluffy Bunny Gang?"

"It's the Animal Adventure Club," said Buzz, taking an angry bite out of his apple.

"Yeah, that's what I meant. Well, I'll see you at the reserve later. Lisa says you'd love to have me in your club. I'll come and help you look for the... What was it? A baby deer?" Lexi babbled. "Aw, they're so cute and cuddly. Like Bambi! When we find it, I'll give it a big squeeze!" She hugged herself and squealed.

Buzz's mouth opened wide. "Lexi, you can't cuddle a fawn. It'd be scared," he explained.

"And if you want to track one, you need to be very *quiet*," said Gracie crossly.

"No problem! *Ssh!*" Lexi whispered, raising a finger to her lips. Just then, she saw someone she knew across the playground. She put her thumb and finger into her mouth and let out a deafening whistle. Isla, Buzz and Gracie covered their ears. Lexi winked and ran off. "See you later!"

"She's so loud!" groaned Gracie.

"And she doesn't know anything about animals," muttered Buzz. "She's *not* joining!"

"Remember our club code?" said Isla. "*We will always welcome new members.*"

Buzz and Gracie sighed.

"OK, let's give her a chance," said Gracie.

"I suppose her whistling might come in handy," said Buzz.

"Yeah, if we need to round up some lost sheep!" laughed Isla.

3

"Isla, do you have your torch?" Buzz asked his friend later that afternoon at the rangers' lodge.

"Check," said Isla, feeling for it in her jacket pocket.

"Map?"

"Check," said Isla.

"I've got mine too. And what are you bringing, Buzz?" Gracie said playfully.

"My torch and map… and biscuits of course!" said Buzz with a smile. "Check!" he added, whipping out a packet of chocolate digestives from his rucksack.

"I wonder what happened to Lexi?"

asked Isla. Although she had reminded her friends about welcoming new members, part of Isla hoped Lexi had changed her mind about coming.

"Hmm," said Buzz. "Maybe she couldn't make it after all."

Just then, the door opened and in came Lisa, the head ranger. "Good afternoon, Animal Adventure Club!" she called.

"Hi Lisa," they all chanted back.

Bouncing in behind her came Lexi, munching on a bag of sweets. "Hi guys!" she bellowed. "I bet you were worried I wasn't coming! I totally forgot." She shrugged. "But Lisa came to pick me up and then I didn't have time to change."

Isla noticed Lexi was wearing a denim jacket and thin sparkly trainers. The other club members were wearing

waterproof jackets and sturdy walking boots. It was meant to rain later. *Lexi's going to get wet feet,* she thought.

"There's a spare anorak hanging over there, Lexi," said Lisa. "It might be a bit big, but it'll do. And there are a lot of muddy paths on the reserve. I don't have any waterproof boots you can borrow, but we'll get you a pair for next time."

Buzz and Gracie were looking annoyed, so Isla decided to try to make Lexi feel welcome. "You're just in time, Lexi," she said. "We're heading off to check on the fawn."

"The what?" mumbled Lexi, her mouth full of pink gunge.

"The baby deer, remember?" said Gracie. "The cute, cuddly Bambi?"

"Oh yeah!" said Lexi, grabbing the anorak. "I forgot about that too!"

Isla spotted Gracie rolling her eyes behind Lexi's back.

"Let me know how you get on tracking it," said Lisa. "There was no sign of it when I was up there earlier. From your description, I would say it was a roe deer fawn. You did an amazing job rescuing it yesterday, but don't get too close again. Just keep an eye out and report back to me. The doe will be close by. Fawns hide while their mums forage for food."

Isla, Buzz and Gracie nodded, and the trio headed for the door, with Lexi trailing behind.

"Enjoy your patrol, Animal Adventure Club!" called Lisa. "While you're out, I'm going to check on Spiky. I hope those nasty ear mites are all gone."

"I think he's feeling better," said Buzz. "His food bowl was nearly empty."

"You can refill it when you get back," Lisa said, smiling. "I'll see you later!"

4

The Animal Adventure Club stepped outside the rangers' lodge and set off towards Loch Dooey.

"Wait a second," said Gracie, signalling for them to be quiet. "Listen to this, Lexi. The blue tit chicks are cheeping again. They're in the nesting box on the wall."

Sure enough, they could hear the faint sounds of hungry birds.

"And look, there's the mum!" said Buzz. A blue tit with a fat caterpillar in her beak was watching from the branches of a nearby tree. She cocked her head to one side.

"I think we're making her nervous. She wants us to move on so she can feed her babies," whispered Isla. They swiftly moved away from the box and the mum swooped in and popped through the tiny hole. The chicks' cheeping became frantic as their mum gave them their dinner.

"Remember we need to top up the bird feeders when we get back, so they've got plenty of food," said Buzz.

Lexi had her hands clamped over her ears. "What a racket!" she shouted, walking away.

"Let me get this right. Lexi thinks *the birds* are loud?" Gracie muttered to Buzz, and he giggled.

"So, Lexi," said Isla brightly, catching up to her. "We're going to Craggy Woods first. Would you like a map so you can get to know your way around?" Isla pulled one out of her pocket.

"A map?" said Lexi. "Nah. Thanks, but I don't need one. I've been here a gazillion times already." She sauntered ahead towards Dooey Burn Bridge, dropping a sweetie wrapper as she went.

"Er, Lexi?" said Buzz, bending down to pick up the wrapper.

Lexi turned round and her face fell. "Oh, I'm sorry," she said, with a look of horror. She pulled out the packet of sweets from her pocket. "I've not even offered you one!"

"Oh no, that's OK," said Buzz. "I meant—"

"The orange ones are my favourites," she said, pushing the bag into Buzz's hand. "Try one!"

"No thanks," he said. Isla and Gracie shook their heads too.

Lexi shrugged, looking a little hurt, and pushed the bag back in her pocket. "Suit yourselves," she said.

There was a gate just over the bridge, which led to the woodland paths. Lexi held it open so they could all walk through.

"Thanks," said Gracie, but then Lexi walked away without closing the gate behind her. "Lexi, you're meant to close gates when you're out in the countryside..." she said. But Lexi was striding ahead and took no notice. Gracie sighed and ran back to swing the gate shut.

"I *love* nature," Lexi announced, marching onwards.

"So," began Buzz, in his best trying-to-make-an-effort-voice, "what's your favourite woodland animal?"

"Ooh... red squirrels," said Lexi.

"Cool," said Buzz. "I like them too. Have you ever seen one?"

"You're kidding, right? Of course I've seen one!" She guffawed loudly and gave Buzz a friendly thump on the arm. "I've seen hundreds!"

Buzz grimaced. "Really? They're actually pretty rare."

"We did a red squirrel watch last year," said Isla, "and we hardly saw any."

"They're *everywhere*!" Lexi chuckled. "You just have to look up, guys!"

Isla was about to argue back, but it was hard to get a word in because Lexi wouldn't stop talking. She told them about all the animals she'd seen and how much of a countryside expert she was. Isla glanced over at Buzz and Gracie, who were walking alongside them with their arms tightly folded. She knew they were feeling annoyed.

They walked on through Craggy Woods until they got back to the wire fence where they'd rescued the trapped fawn.

"Why are we stopping here?" asked Lexi.

"To check for the fawn, remember?" reminded Buzz.

Lexi frowned and plonked herself down on a tree stump. "Och well, I'll just have a wee rest," she said and pulled out her bag of sweets.

The others began walking around, scanning the area. "Well, there's no sign of it lying injured, which is a good thing," said Isla.

"Guys!" yelled Gracie. "Come and see this!"

Isla and Buzz rushed over to Gracie, who was standing by a tall Scots pine tree.

"Is that what I think it is?" Gracie said, pointing to a smear of something dark and sticky on the bark. Isla knelt down for a better look. Buzz touched it lightly and his fingers came away red.

"It's blood," confirmed Buzz.

"Ew!" squealed Lexi.

"And at the same height as the fawn's neck," said Gracie.

"Maybe the fawn was more badly injured than we thought," said Isla. "Come on, let's look for more clues."

5

Determined to find the injured fawn, the Animal Adventure Club crept further into Craggy Woods.

"It gets pretty dark in the middle of a forest, doesn't it?" said Lexi, still chewing her sweets. "We won't be able to see much later on."

"That's why we brought our torches," sighed Buzz, snatching up another sweetie wrapper Lexi had dropped on the forest floor. He stuffed it into his pocket and glared at Lexi, who was walking on ahead.

The low afternoon sun shone through the trees and on to a carpet of spring bluebells.

"Those flowers are gorgeous! I bet Lisa would love a bunch to brighten up the rangers' lodge," said Lexi, trampling through the patch of bluebells and bending down to pluck a few from the forest floor.

"Stop!" shrieked Gracie. Everyone jumped.

Isla looked over to Lexi, who was frozen

in shock, her fist clenched around the clump of delicate flowers.

"What is it? Are they... *poisonous*?" whispered Lexi, almost too scared to move.

"I think Gracie was trying to say that you shouldn't pick wildflowers, Lexi," said Isla gently.

Lexi frowned at Gracie, let go of the flowers and stood up. "You gave me a real fright," she said.

"I didn't mean to shout," said Gracie, "but you shouldn't do that."

Isla threw Gracie a look that meant 'Don't say any more!' But it didn't work.

"Wildflowers are for everyone to enjoy," Gracie added, folding her arms.

"Well, I didn't know, OK?" Lexi's face flushed bright red and she glared angrily at Gracie. "I just thought Lisa would like them. You shouldn't shout at people, Gracie."

Isla could see tears brimming in Lexi's eyes and she suddenly felt sorry for her.

"I'm going back to the lodge," Lexi huffed, and she turned around and stomped off through the trees.

"Come back, Lexi!" shouted Isla. "We didn't mean to upset you!"

But Lexi didn't reply.

"Maybe we should just let her go," muttered Buzz. "She'll cool off."

"No, we have to go after her," said Isla.

"Ugh!" said Gracie, shaking her head. "Me and my big mouth. I'll go and say sorry."

Isla put her hand on her friend's arm. "We'll *all* go after her, Gracie. We'll make it right. Come on."

They followed the path that Lexi had taken.

"If she's going to the lodge, she's set off in the wrong direction," said Buzz.

"Hey, wait," said Gracie. "Look at this." She pointed to a patch of soft mud. "Prints!" she said.

"Lexi's?" asked Buzz.

"No, the fawn's," said Gracie. "They're deer hoofprints, or 'slots' to be exact. And they're going in the opposite direction to Lexi."

They gathered round and looked carefully at the small curved prints on the ground.

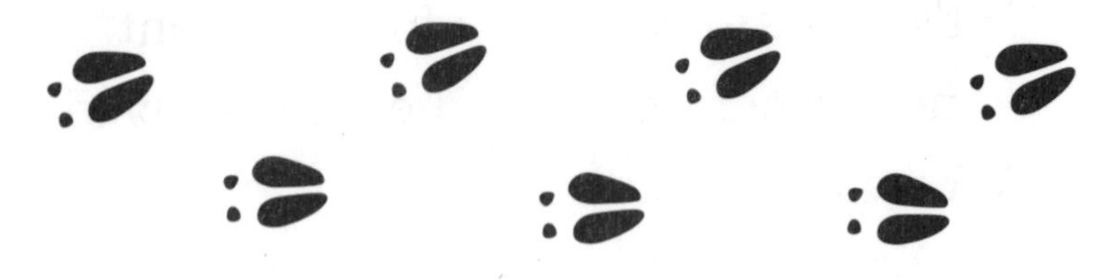

"I don't think these slots have been here long," said Gracie excitedly. "The fawn might be close by!"

"In that case, I think we need to follow the tracks," said Isla. "If the fawn is still bleeding, it could need help. We can keep looking for Lexi afterwards."

The others nodded in agreement. Isla signalled to them to keep as quiet as possible, so they didn't scare off the injured fawn.

"Here!" whispered Buzz, shining his torch towards a patch of red on a branch of a small tree. "More blood!"

"It must be *very* close," murmured Isla. "Let's keep still and quiet for a moment."

They stood listening. The trees swayed and creaked in the breeze, and from the treetops they could hear the joyful call of a chaffinch. Isla scanned all around them.

If I were an injured fawn, where would I go? Isla thought to herself. *Somewhere I couldn't be seen, of course. I wouldn't want to be found. Where would I be camouflaged if I had light-coloured fur and darker spots?*

There was a faint rustling nearby, and a slight movement caught Isla's eye. She peered over to a patch of dried leaves. *I'd hide in fallen leaves!* She tapped Buzz and Gracie on their arms and pointed.

There, curled up against a tree, was the fawn. With the dried leaves as a nest, it was almost completely hidden. They could just make out its soft downy fur, dappled body, large velvet ears and shiny black nose.

"Aw, poor wee thing," gasped Gracie.

"I can see a cut on its neck," murmured Buzz. "What are we going to do?"

"Remember what Lisa said: we can't go too near," warned Isla. "Its mother might be nearby. And we really shouldn't interfere."

"But if we leave it here, it'll be in danger from other animals. An injured fawn would be easy to catch," whispered Buzz.

"I think there's another animal around already," said Gracie, crouching down. "Look at these."

Buzz and Isla looked into the soft mud and saw another set of prints. Isla thought they looked familiar. "Wait a second," she said, taking her notepad out of her rucksack and flipping it open to a drawing. "Gracie, these prints look just like ones that I found in my garden. I drew them to show you. I thought they belonged to..."

"A fox!" Gracie whispered.

She moved forward to look at Isla's picture of the pawprints and stepped on a large branch. It snapped loudly. Spooked, the fawn bounded up and shot away into the trees ahead.

"Oh no!" groaned Gracie. "First it was my big mouth and now it's my stupid big feet!"

"Don't be hard on yourself, Gracie," said Isla kindly, putting her arm around her friend's shoulder. "At least we know the fawn can run away from predators."

"We can't risk leaving it this time, though," said Buzz, shaking his head. "The fawn has a cut on its neck, and it may need stitches and medicine to stop any infection."

"And we know there's definitely a fox around, so the fawn is in danger from that too," said Gracie.

"We'd better hurry back to the lodge," said Isla. "This time we really do need Lisa's help."

6

"Lisa?" called Buzz as the Animal Adventure Club all tumbled into the rangers' lodge.

Lisa was holding Spiky and peering into his ears.

"Yay! You're back!" she said cheerfully. "Two seconds, I'm just giving Spiky his last dose of ear drops. He's looking great!"

"Lisa, it's the fawn," blurted Gracie. "We saw a nasty cut on its neck and we think it's badly injured, but then I stood on a branch and it ran off."

"Whoa!" said Lisa. "Slow down, Gracie." She popped Spiky back in his cage, took off her gloves and came over to the group. She frowned. "Hey, wait a minute, where's Lexi?"

"Er... We thought she was with you," stammered Isla.

"She said she was coming back to the lodge," said Buzz.

"You let her come back by herself?" asked Lisa quietly. "She wouldn't know the way."

Isla, Buzz and Gracie looked at each other awkwardly.

"But she stormed off," said Gracie. "She left the gate open, and she was picking wildflowers. I told her she shouldn't."

"*And* she was dropping sweetie wrappers," added Buzz. "I had to pick them up."

"We tried to stop her," said Isla.

Lisa frowned and folded her arms.

A guilty silence hung over the children. Isla knew that they weren't telling Lisa the whole truth.

"But maybe we didn't try hard enough," said Isla, chewing her thumbnail.

Gracie looked down at her feet. "It *was* sort of my fault," she muttered. "I think I upset her. I got a bit, well... angry."

Lisa didn't need to say anything. The children knew from her face that she was disappointed. She grabbed her jacket and swung it round her shoulders.

"Look," she said, "I know Lexi can sometimes put her foot in it and say the wrong thing. *Loudly*," she added, with a twinkle in her eye. "The thing is, it's all a bit of an act. Between you and me, she was really nervous before we came today. That's why we were late. She had changed her mind and wasn't going to come, but I persuaded her. I said I knew you would make her feel welcome."

Isla shifted her feet uncomfortably. She could feel her face getting very hot.

"But why didn't she want to come?" asked Buzz.

"She was a bit scared. Behind all that

confidence, Lexi is shy. She's only been in Pittendooey for a few weeks and it's very hard to move to a small town when you don't know a soul. It's not easy fitting in. Remember, you've all known each other forever! Well, at least since nursery."

Buzz, Gracie and Isla glanced at each other guiltily.

"She's just been trying too hard. Can you give her a chance?" asked Lisa.

The children nodded.

"We're really sorry," said Isla.

"We'll make it up to her," Gracie promised.

"Well, we need to find her first," said Lisa, opening the door of the lodge. "Now, what about the fawn. Did you actually see it?"

"Yes, curled up under a tree in Dritchel Woods, but it ran off," said Gracie.

"And before that, we found more patches of blood," added Buzz.

Lisa glanced at her watch. "Right, it's 5 p.m. now, so we need to find Lexi before it gets late. At least it won't get dark for a while. I'll check Craggy Woods, and keep my eyes open for the fawn too. Sounds like it's not too badly injured if it's up and about," Lisa reassured them. "I'm sure its mother will be nearby and looking out for it. But if I need to, I can call my friend the vet at the wildlife hospital in Strathdooey. You follow the path the other way, towards the boat sheds, to look for Lexi," she said, setting off towards Dooey Burn Bridge.

"I hope Lexi's found her way onto the path," said Buzz as they walked around the east side of Loch Dooey. "Then at least we'll meet her as she comes round the loch."

"I don't have a good feeling about this," said Isla. "She was *very* upset when she left us."

Dark clouds filled the sky as they walked along, and a few spots of rain quickly turned into a shower. They all pulled up their hoods and trudged on through the gloom.

"Lexi!" yelled Gracie, her eyes wide and anxious. "Where are you? Lexi!"

Her voice echoed around the reserve. They all stopped walking and stood silently, listening. The rain was falling heavily now, pattering on the surface of the loch in a million tiny round ripples. The wind was picking up too. There was no reply, only the distant cry of an oyster catcher.

"Where is she?" said Buzz, sounding panicky. "What are we going to do?"

7

"Come on, guys!" said Isla, putting her arms around Gracie and Buzz. "We're the Animal Adventure Club, remember? What do our club rules say about problems?"

Buzz sniffed and wiped a drop of rain from the end of his nose. "'We will deal with problems calmly...'"

"'...and come up with a sensible plan,'" finished Gracie, grinning. "You're right, Isla, we can do this!"

Standing together in the pouring rain, Gracie, Buzz and Isla nodded and gave each other a small, wet fist bump.

"So," said Isla, "I've got an idea. Gracie, what would you do if you were tracking an animal?"

"First I would look for signs," Gracie began.

"What sort of signs?" asked Buzz.

"Well, the obvious ones, like footprints or tracks. But other things too, like animal fur or feathers caught on fences, or chew marks."

"OK, that's a good start. What else?" said Isla as they continued walking.

"I suppose I would try to *think* like that animal," Gracie said. "So I'd try to guess what the animal might do and where it might go."

"Right," said Buzz. "So we need to think like Lexi. Where *might* she have gone after she left us?"

"Remember, she was heading out of Dritchel Woods, but not on the main path," said Isla. "She might have come up and over the old Roman fort remains."

"And if she did that, then she'd have gone down the hill towards the Boggy Burn," Gracie continued.

"And then she would have ended up in Barleycorn Forest!" finished Buzz. "Why don't we try heading down the hill towards the burn and see if we can find any clues. Then we'll know if we're on the right lines." They all nodded in agreement.

Feeling more focussed, Isla, Buzz and Gracie moved away from the path around the loch towards the Boggy Burn. It was very soft and sticky underfoot. The rain was pelting on their hoods now and they carefully scanned the ground as they walked.

Although Isla was worried about Lexi, she couldn't help thinking about the injured fawn. She remembered it curled up in the leaves, frightened. Like Lexi, the fawn might be cold and all alone. *We must keep an eye out for it,* she thought, *while we're looking for Lexi.* It could easily have wandered over to this part of the reserve.

"Aha!" shouted Buzz, snapping Isla out of her thoughts. He pointed to something

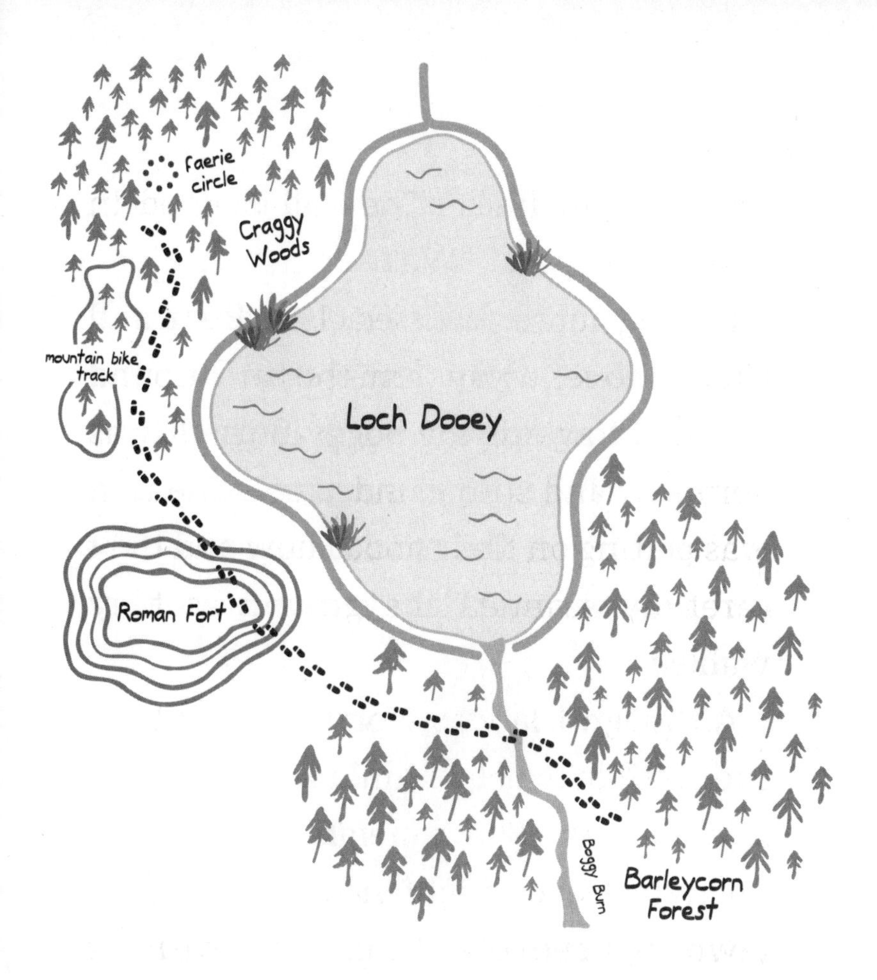

shiny on the ground. They quickly gathered round as Buzz picked up the object. "It's a sweetie wrapper!" He reached into his pocket to pull out one of the sweetie wrappers he'd picked up earlier.

"It's the same. It's Lexi's all right!"

"Good," said Isla. "We're on her trail."

"Yup," said Gracie. "And what's this?" She reached down and began heaving at something sparkly stuck in the boggy ground. With a loud sucking noise, she pulled it out of the mud. "Lexi's trainer! I recognise the sparkles even under all that mud!"

"Oh no," said Isla. "Poor Lexi only has one shoe!"

Gracie peered closely at the ground and said, "Look at this!" There was a clear set of tracks: a shoe print followed by a bare foot. "She went this way."

The Animal Adventure Club set off quickly, following the footprint trail until they were on the edge of Barleycorn Forest. Someone had left the gate wide open. They looked at each other.

"We're *definitely* on the right path," said Gracie.

Barleycorn Forest was on the other side of the reserve from Craggy Woods, and much larger. The trees stood closer together, which made it feel very dark and a little scary. The footprints led them up towards one of the nature trails that wound through the forest, but then they stopped.

"Hmm," said Gracie. "There are no more footprints now because the path is gravel."

"She's going to have a sore foot from walking on these stones," said Buzz. "They're pretty sharp."

"Which way now? Should we split up into two search parties?" asked Isla, with a touch of doubt in her voice. "She could have turned left or right down the path. In two groups, we can cover both directions."

"But then one of us would be left alone," said Gracie.

"Maybe we should call Lisa," said Buzz, pulling his phone out of his pocket. "Uh oh, there's no signal in this part of the forest."

Isla pulled down her hood and scratched her head, letting the rain soak her hair. The sky was grey and dull, and the wind howled through the trees. She was nervous and could tell from Buzz's frown and Gracie's clenched fists that they felt the same. None of them were sure what to do.

But suddenly, from deep in the middle of Barleycorn Forest, came a long wail.

"What was that?" exclaimed Isla.

"It came from over there!" cried Gracie. She pointed to the right. Without saying another word, the Animal Adventure Club set off, running into the depths of the forest.

8

Isla, Buzz and Gracie crept through the trees and bracken. They stepped over roots and weaved around tree trunks, towards the mysterious wailing sound. They took out their torches and used them to scan the dark forest floor.

"Look, there are some slots!" said Gracie. "Just like the fawn's tracks we saw earlier on."

"And human prints too: a shoe and a foot!" said Buzz.

"And they're both headed in the same direction!" cried Isla.

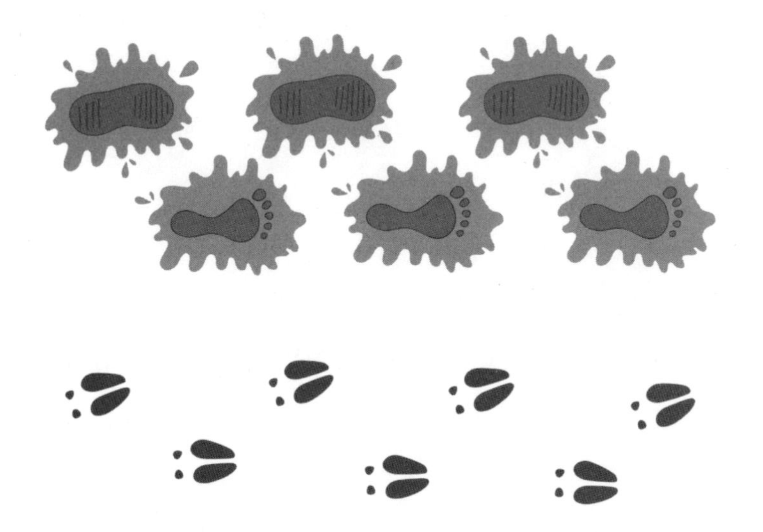

They walked on cautiously.

"Here!" said Gracie. Flashing the torches towards the trees, they could clearly see grass and branches flattened and broken. Once again they heard the low moan. They all froze in terror.

"L-L-L-Lexi?" stammered Buzz. "Is that y-y-y-you?"

They listened. Isla could feel her heart pounding in her chest.

"Help!" came a desperate cry. It was Lexi's voice.

"We're coming, Lexi," they all yelled in terror and relief.

"Shout again so we can find you!" called Buzz.

"I'm over here!" she wailed.

"Do that amazing whistle you can do," yelled Gracie, "then we can follow the sound."

They followed the whistle and trampled further into the dark forest, pushing branches out of the way, and then, suddenly, they saw her. Lying crumpled in a deep, muddy ditch was a dishevelled and tearful Lexi. She was filthy and soaking wet, and her legs were covered in cuts.

"I couldn't see where I was going," she said, her teeth chattering. She shaded her eyes against the torchlight. "And then I slipped."

"You're shivering!" said Isla.

"It... was... s-s-sunny... and d-dry... when I arrived at the reserve." Lexi's teeth rattled. "B-but now it's wet and f-f-f-f-freezing. I should have... worn... more... clothes. Even the a-a-a-norak Lisa g-gave me is s-s-soaking now. S-so s-s-s-s-stupid of me."

"Let's get you out of the ditch," said Isla.

"I think I've d-done s-s-something to my ankle," chittered Lexi. "I... c-can't... get... up."

Awkwardly, Gracie and Isla each took one of Lexi's arms over their shoulders, while Buzz helped guide them out of the muddy hole and up onto the forest floor.

"And there's s-s-something watching me!" Lexi added, sounding terrified. "There's s-s-something in the trees over there!"

Buzz, Isla and Gracie shot each other a confused look. They sat Lexi carefully on an old moss-covered tree stump.

"I've got your other shoe here," said Gracie, offering it to Lexi.

"I couldn't get it out of the bog," said Lexi, reaching out with a muddy hand.

"I don't think there's much point trying to put it on," said Buzz, examining Lexi's foot. "Your ankle's really swollen and I don't think you'll be able to walk. We'll need to carry you back. Here, have a biscuit for the shock." He whipped out the chocolate digestives from his rucksack.

"I'm so sorry!" Lexi howled, waving the biscuits away with her hands. "I should've listened to you. And I've been so frightened!"

"It's OK," said Buzz, trying to calm her down, and then popping a biscuit into his own mouth instead. "We'd have found you eventually," he said, munching.

"At least by morning," teased Isla, giving Lexi a wink. "And we're sorry we let you go off on your own."

"I shouldn't have shouted at you," admitted Gracie. I'm really sorry too."

Lexi smiled weakly and wiped her nose with the back of her hand. "Thanks guys," she said.

"I'll send Lisa a text to let her know that we've found you," said Buzz, his mouth full of crumbs. He glanced at his phone. "Oh, I forgot there was no signal! Never mind, we'll be back at the lodge soon enough."

Lexi began wailing again.

"There's nothing to be scared of, Lexi," said Isla, putting her arm around her. "You're safe now."

Lexi pointed ahead. "I'm telling you.

Over there. It's like we're being watched! I think it's a g-g-g-ghost!"

Buzz stopped crunching biscuits. They all listened. Some way off, they could hear the eerie cawing of a flock of rooks high in the trees. The branches all around them creaked. Isla shivered.

"I'm sure it's just your imagination playing tricks on you, Lexi," said Gracie, sounding a little spooked. "You've had a real fright. Once we get you back to the lodge, you'll be fine."

But then they heard a snapping of twigs and movement in the undergrowth.

"What was that?" said Buzz, shining his torch in the direction of the sound. Suddenly, out of the shadows, two gleaming eyes shone back at them.

They all gasped.

"I think Lexi's right," said Isla quietly. "Something is watching... but I don't think it's watching *us!*"

9

Lexi peered around the dark wood, her eyes wide with fright. "What do you think is out there, Isla?"

"I think it's a fox, just like the one in my garden. I saw a flash of its long nose and whiskers when Buzz shone his torch."

"A fox!" Lexi was clearly terrified.

"But why is it watching us?" asked Gracie.

"Well, that's just it," said Isla. "There must be something here that the fox is interested in, otherwise it would have run away from us. I think it knows there's prey nearby – which means there's an animal in danger."

"The fawn!" gasped Gracie. "Remember we saw its tracks when we spotted Lexi's footprints? It must be round here somewhere!"

The Animal Adventure Club stood back to back and stepped around in a circle very carefully, scanning the ground. But it was Lexi who spotted something first, from her spot on the tree stump.

"Buzz, shine your light back over there," she whispered, pointing to a pile of leaves and branches a little way off.

Buzz flashed his torch. "I don't think anything's there," he said.

"Perhaps it's something that doesn't *want* to be found," said Isla, remembering how the injured fawn had camouflaged itself in Craggy Woods. "I think you're right, Lexi."

They all peered at the torchlit spot and soon they noticed the leaves twitch.

"Oh my goodness!" said Gracie, trying not to speak too loudly. "It *is* the fawn!"

Once again they saw the baby deer lying down, almost concealed by fallen leaves. This time, it was staring right at them. Isla could see its chest rising and falling quickly. It was breathing rapidly.

"It looks really frightened and tired," whispered Isla. "I hope it's OK."

"Wow," murmured Lexi. "I've never seen anything like it in real life before. It's amazing."

Buzz moved the torchlight away. "I don't want to spook it again."

"Don't worry, I'll not be stepping on any branches this time," said Gracie.

"Was it following me?" asked Lexi in a quiet voice. "Why would it do that?"

"I don't know," said Isla. "Maybe it thought you might protect it until its mother found it."

"Can't we try to pick it up and take it back to the lodge?" asked Lexi. "If we leave it here, the fox will get it."

"No," said Isla, shaking her head. "We definitely must not touch it. I know I got close rescuing it from the fence, but that was a bit different. Lisa was really clear: we mustn't move it or scare it off this time. The doe must be somewhere nearby."

"She's probably looking for her wee one right now," added Buzz.

"It's all my fault," Lexi muttered. "It followed me for safety, and now the minute we move away the fox will grab it."

"It's not your fault, Lexi," said Buzz. "But... yeah, the hungry fox sees the fawn as supper, that's for sure."

"We need to get some help. Lisa will know what to do," said Isla, taking out her phone.

"No signal here, remember!" Gracie reminded her.

"I'll stay here and guard the fawn," said Lexi firmly. "And you go and get Lisa. I owe it to the fawn to help it. *I'm not leaving.*"

Isla turned and stared at Lexi. In the shadows, she was sitting quite still, with her arms folded. She wasn't shouting or snorting or being loud. She was being calm and sensible. *She's thinking about what's best for the fawn,* Isla realised.

"We're not leaving you alone," said Isla. "I'll stay too." She took Lexi's hand in her own.

With a firm nod, Buzz and Gracie turned and made their way back out of Barleycorn Forest, leaving the two girls behind to guard the fawn.

10

Lexi turned to Isla. "Do you think the fawn is lonely? And frightened?"

Isla didn't say anything at first. She just held Lexi's hand and put her coat around their shoulders to keep them warm. The girls sat cosied up together, facing the fawn's hiding place. It had stopped raining now but it still felt quite dark, sitting amongst all the trees.

"I think it must be," Lexi continued. "I know exactly how it feels." Even through the gloom Isla could make out large tears rolling down Lexi's cheeks.

"It's going to be OK," soothed Isla.

“Try not to worry. We won’t let anything get it.”

“I’ve never been out in the middle of a dark forest,” said Lexi. “If I’m scared, just imagine how the fawn feels!” At every sound and rustle, Lexi tensed and shut her eyes, burying her head into her chest.

"Actually," said Isla, "I'm quite enjoying myself!"

Lexi turned and looked at Isla, her mouth wide open in surprise.

Isla gave Lexi a friendly nudge. "It's all about how you look at something. You see it as a bit dark and scary. But I think it's exciting to be here with so many animals. Actually, we're not alone at all. We're really, really lucky!"

Just then, they heard a sound that made Lexi grip Isla's hand tight.

"Did you hear that?" Isla gasped.

"Yes," Lexi muttered, her face buried in the wet anorak. "It sounded like something scary!"

"Shh, listen."

A bird called softly and Lexi looked up.

"Cuckoo." She copied the sound.

"Is it really a cuckoo?" she asked. "I've never heard one before."

"Yes," said Isla. "Do you know they lay their eggs in other birds' nests?"

"Cheeky things!" said Lexi. Suddenly she spotted something in the bracken. "What's that brown, furry thing over there?" She clutched at Isla and pointed. "It's not a r-r-rat, is it?"

The creature bounded into the clearing and sniffed the air. Then, sensing it wasn't alone, it bounded away.

"Phew," breathed Lexi. "Just a silly old rabbit."

"A little bit cuter than a rat," whispered Isla. "There might be a rabbit warren beneath us. They're amazing - lots of different tunnels and cosy little nesting rooms. And escape routes!"

"It's lucky the fox didn't go after the rabbit," said Lexi.

"I suppose it's got its eye on something bigger," said Isla, and the girls were quiet for a moment.

"You really do know so much, Isla," said Lexi, in awe of her new friend. She paused and then said, "Can I tell you something? You know I said I'd seen loads of red squirrels... Well, that was a bit of a fib. I hadn't really seen one before." Lexi looked at Isla, her eyes shining. "That is until this evening! When I fell in the ditch, I was feeling really sorry for myself – but then I saw a red squirrel run up a tree! It was so cute. Much cuter than I'd thought it would be."

"That's amazing, Lexi, you're so lucky! But *why* did you lie to us before?" asked Isla quietly.

"I suppose I wanted to impress you all by making you think I knew tons about animals," said Lexi. "Lisa told me about the Animal Adventure Club and it sounded so much fun I wanted to be part of it too. I don't have many friends, really. I've been a wee bit lonely since we moved to Pittendooey."

"You don't need to impress us, Lexi. I like you just the way you are. And you know a lot more about animals now!" said Isla. Lexi smiled back at her.

Just then there was a scuffling noise.

"It's the fox," whispered Isla.

They could just make out the fox's silhouette. It was skulking out from its hiding place into the clearing.

"Oh no," said Lexi. "It's moving towards the fawn. What should we do?"

"Now it's my turn to tell the truth," said Isla. "*I have no idea!* I didn't think it would come close while we were sitting here. But foxes can be bold."

Lexi grabbed Isla's arm. "I've got an idea! Do you have a torch?"

"Yes!" she said. "Here, in my pocket." She pulled it out and handed it to Lexi.

"This might just work," said Lexi, switching the torch on. She shone the beam directly at the fox. Its eyes lit up like two bright stars and, sure enough, it froze.

"Go on," Lexi shooed. "Away you go."

Uncertain, the fox stood still for a moment or two, staring at them. Isla didn't dare breathe. Just then came the sound of pounding steps bounding in their direction. Something was winding its way through the trees towards them and then they heard a low, rasping bark. For the first time that evening, it was Isla who gripped Lexi's arm. "What now?" she whispered.

The girls clung together as suddenly, jumping into the clearing on long, graceful legs, came a doe! It let out two short barks. Alarmed, the fox turned and bolted deep into the trees.

"Amazing!" Isla said quietly. "That's the fawn's mother, come to save the day!"

The doe trotted over to her baby and nudged it tenderly. The fawn stood up and its mother immediately began to groom it with tender licks. But then something extraordinary happened. The fawn walked slowly towards the girls. Lexi shone the torch to one side so as not

to dazzle it. It came closer and closer and stared. Its heavy breath puffed from its nostrils.

"Wow," whispered Lexi. "I can't believe what I'm seeing."

"It's a roe deer doe, and I think it's thanking you, Lexi!" said Isla.

"Thanking both of us." Lexi smiled.

The fawn continued to stare with its huge, glassy eyes and then suddenly, with a shake of its head, let out an enormous sneeze! Both girls jumped and then burst out laughing. And then its mother wandered close to them too.

"Well, the fawn isn't bleeding anymore," said Isla, taking the torch and shining the light on the soft fur of its neck. "The injury isn't as bad as we'd thought. It's healing up. Its mum seems happy too."

And, with a nod from its mother, the fawn turned away. Together, they leapt off through the trees, the white tufts of their bottoms bouncing further and further into the depths of Barleycorn Forest.

"This has turned into the most amazing night *ever!*" said Lexi. "I've seen a red squirrel, a fox, a rabbit, a roe deer doe and its fawn, and a cuckoo."

"We should do this again!" laughed Isla.

"Well, minus the falling-in-the-ditch part!" chuckled Lexi, shaking her head.

"Isla! Lexi!" They heard Buzz's voice call out. "Are you OK?"

"We're fantastic!" Lexi shouted back joyfully.

11

"Who wants hot chocolate?" asked Buzz as they arrived back at the lodge.

"Oh yes please," said Lexi, hobbling in with Lisa and Isla's help. "I'd drink hot mud if it would warm me up!"

"Would you like marshmallows with your mud, madam?" asked Buzz in a silly voice as he searched the cupboards for cups and spoons.

The Animal Adventure Club hung up their wet jackets and they all sat by the stove. Gracie carefully helped Lexi put her leg up on the coffee table and Lisa fetched an ice pack from the freezer to put on her swollen ankle. Isla put a blanket around Lexi's shoulders.

"Sorry we sent you out on a wild-goose chase, Lisa," said Isla. "All the excitement was at the other end of the reserve."

"Don't worry about it," said Lisa. "I'm just so pleased that you found Lexi and the fawn! Good work, Animal Adventure Club."

Lexi glanced around. "Well, it wasn't good work from me," she mumbled.

"I caused you lots of trouble. I was really silly and I'm so sorry." She gave a great sigh. "Oh dear."

Isla caught Gracie's eye and they both began to smile. Then Isla looked at Buzz, whose shoulders were shaking. Isla let out a snort. She couldn't keep it in any longer. They all started laughing. Lexi looked confused.

"Oh dear. *Oh deer!* Get it?" chortled Isla. "Lexi, I never knew you were so funny!"

Lexi looked at them all, confused. "But that's not what I meant... Oh, I keep making mistakes!"

"Don't take it so hard, Lexi. We *all* make mistakes – and some of them are funny," chuckled Lisa. "Listen, I've got an idea that'll make you feel better: why not help other people learn from your mistakes?"

"What do you mean?" asked Lexi.

"Why don't you make a poster or fact sheet? Something for our visitors to read," suggested Lisa. "And you could illustrate it. You're really good at drawing. You won that prize, remember?"

"Wow, that's amazing!" said Isla. "And a fact sheet was on our list of jobs to do. That would be perfect."

Lexi went a deep shade of red. "But I don't deserve to be a member of the Animal Adventure Club," she said.

"Yes you do!" blurted Gracie.

"You really cared about that wee fawn, Lexi," added Isla. "You were so brave and you scared the fox away. You saved the baby deer's life!"

"It's official," said Buzz, writing on the Animal Adventure Club's notice board.

"I've added your name to the list of members."

Isla saw a tear in Lexi's eye.

"Thanks everyone," Lexi said. "I'll do my best. And I'll make some fact sheets too – though I'll need some help from you all. I don't know that much about animals."

"No problem," said Gracie. "We'll tell you everything we know!"

"You can start learning about hedgehogs right now," said Lisa, who had taken Spiky out of his cage and was bringing him over to Lexi. "This wee guy's ears are all better now, so we can release him back into the wild tomorrow. Want to help me, Lexi?"

"You bet!" said Lexi, her eyes shining. "Gracie, Buzz, Isla, I hope you'll come too!"

"You're on," said Isla, and Buzz and Gracie smiled and nodded. They all leaned in for their first Animal Adventure Club fist bump as a team of four.

The headlights of a car drawing up outside shone through the window. "That's your mum, Isla," said Lisa.

"See you tomorrow then, to say goodbye to Spiky," Isla said. Then she leaned over and gave Lexi a hug. "You're going to have great fun in the Animal Adventure Club, Lexi. I can't wait!" Then she grabbed her things and bounded out of the lodge, glad to get into her mum's warm car.

"So how was your evening?" asked her mum, as she looked Isla up and down. "What a state you're in, Isla MacLeod!

You look like you've been dragged through a hedge backwards." She picked a bit of twig out of Isla's hair. "What on earth have you been up to?"

Isla grinned. "You'll never guess. Let me tell you all about it..."

ANIMAL ADVENTURE CLUB CODE

MEMBERS:

Isla MacLeod

Buzz (Robert) Campbell

Gracie Munroe

Lexi Budge (newest member!)

OUR MISSION IS TO TAKE CARE OF ALL LIVING CREATURES.

CODE

1. We will treat all animals from bugs to badgers with respect. Even midges and spiders!
2. We will look after the natural world and respect the countryside.
3. We will never drop litter. And we'll recycle any we find lying around.

4. We will have fun outdoors!

5. We will always work as a team.

6. We will deal with problems calmly and come up with a sensible plan.

7. We will ask adults for advice when we need to.

8. We will always be prepared and pack a torch, map, compass and waterproof jacket before going on patrol.

9. We will always welcome new members.

10. We will always have hot chocolate and a packet of biscuits in the lodge.

Preferably custard creams!

SIGNED:

Buzz Isla

Gracie Lexi

How to make a bug hotel

A bug hotel is a great place for beasties to find shelter, especially in autumn and winter. Make one with bits and pieces you find in your garden or on a nature walk.

You will need...

- **plastic drinking bottle** (but if you don't have one, just bundle up the rest of the materials and tie them together with string)
- **hollow plant stems** (bamboo is good, or you can use old garden canes)
- **twigs and sticks**
- **moss**
- **bark**
- **pine cones**
- **sharp scissors**
- **string**

1. Ask a grown-up to cut the top and bottom off the plastic bottle so you have a long tube.

2. Stuff the bottle with all the twigs, sticks, stems and bark. Pack it tightly so nothing falls out. Ask a grown-up to trim or prune any bamboo canes and sticks for you so they fit nicely.

3. Cram all the spaces with the pine cones and moss.

4. Tie some string around the bottle and hang it from the branch of a tree. If you've made a few, stack them up in a nice shady part of the garden.

5. You could even paint a wee 'Bug Hotel' sign on a nice flat pebble.

6. Every so often, have a peek to see which bugs have come to stay!

How to make a footprint trap

Making a footprint trap is a really fun way to find out which animals visit your garden!

You will need...

- large tray (an old baking tray is fine)
- dog or cat food (or bird food like nuts or seeds)
- fine sand
- jug of water
- small bowl
- trowel or spoon

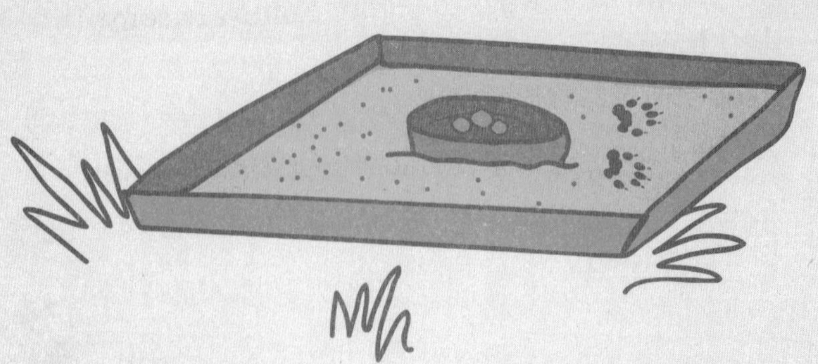

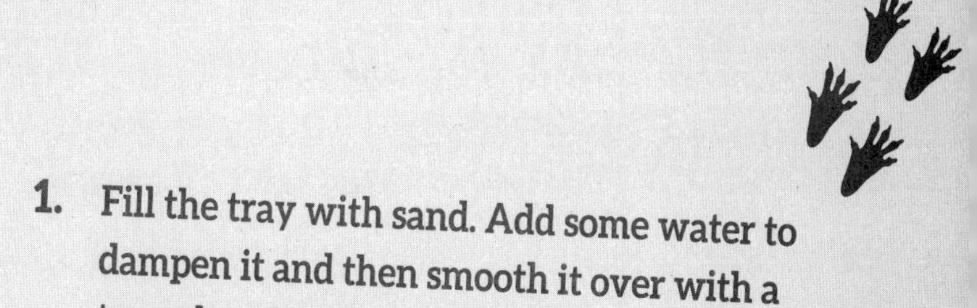

1. Fill the tray with sand. Add some water to dampen it and then smooth it over with a trowel or the back of a spoon.

2. Place your own hand in the sand to make sure it's damp enough to leave a nice clear print. If it doesn't look clear, add a little more water and smooth it over again.

3. Pop the dog, cat or bird food in the bowl and place it in the middle of the tray.

4. Leave the tray in the garden overnight. Good places are beside a bird feeder or next to some low bushes.

5. In the morning, look for footprints in the sand and see if you can identify the animal... or maybe even animals!

Hedgehog

Male = Boar
Female = Sow
Babies = Hoglets

What do we look like?

- When we feel threatened, we roll tightly into a ball so all you can see is prickles.

Hedgehog footprints

Where do we live?

- We can be found all over Britain and Europe.
- We live in hedges, fields, and woodlands.

What do we like to eat?

- We eat beetles, caterpillars, slugs, snails and earthworms.
- Never give us milk or bread, because it's bad for us.
- Instead, give us plenty of fresh water and a bowl of dog or cat food.

Fun facts

- We are nocturnal (we sleep during the day and come out at night).
- You can make your garden 'hog friendly' by leaving some areas a bit wild.
- We have poor eyesight, but we have good hearing and a great sense of smell. We are good swimmers and even climb well too!

Fox

Male = Dog
Female = Vixen
Babies = Cubs or Kits

What do we look like?

- We have reddish coats but our throats and bellies are white or grey.

Where do we live?

- We live in dens all over the world, in the countryside, towns and cities.

What do we like to eat?

- We will eat just about anything, we really like small animals, berries and insects.

What do we sound like?

- We make all sorts of noises and each one means something different.
- We can bark, whine, yelp, shriek, call and growl.

Fun facts

- Foxes are members of the dog family, but we hunt and stalk our prey a bit like a cat.
- Foxes are very good at hunting as we have great eyesight in the dark.
- We also have excellent senses of smell and hearing.
- A group of foxes is called a skulk.

Roe Deer

Male = Buck
Female = Doe
Baby = Fawn

What do we look like?

- We have large ears. Males have small antlers with three points.
- In the summer, our coats are rusty red. In winter, they are grey.
- Our hoof prints are called slots.
- Roe deer don't have tails – we have fluffy white bottoms!

Where do we live?

- We are common in Britain and Europe.
- We live in woodlands.

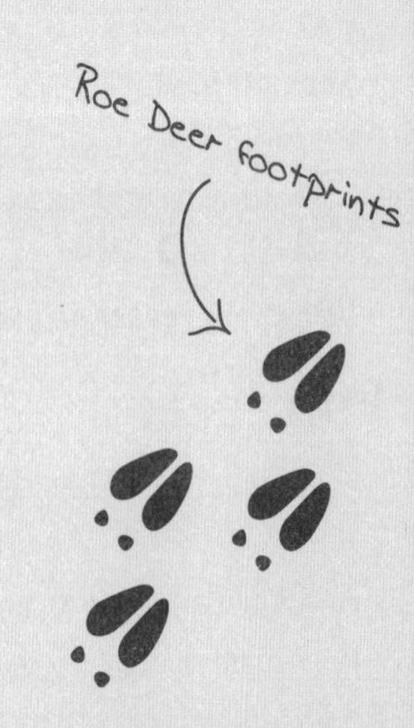

What do we like to eat?

- Plants, young trees, and heather.

What do we sound like?

- We bark when we're anxious.

Fun facts

- We're very shy.
- Bambi was a Roe Deer!

Red Squirrel

Babies = Kittens

What do we look like?

- We have reddish fur, tufty ears and reddish tails.
- Our long bushy tails help us balance as we run along branches.
- Our coats change colour in winter to a dark browny-grey.

Where do we live?

- Our nests are called dreys.
- We are rare in Britain. but you are most likely to spot us in Scotland.
- We are more common in parts of Europe.

What do we like to eat?

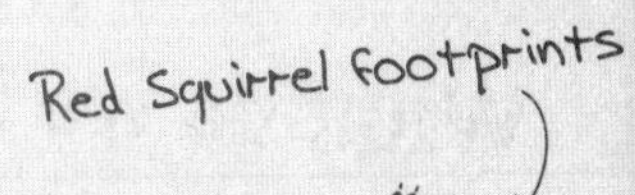

- We love to eat pine seeds, hazelnuts and acorns.

Fun facts

- We don't hibernate in winter.
- We store food in the autumn for when we're less active in winter.
- We're both right- and left-handed when we hold our food.
- We're great swimmers.
- We're very rare, and quite shy too.

What if I find an injured wild animal?

The Animal Adventure Club have lots of exciting encounters with wild animals, but remember that in real life you should always ask a grown-up for help. If you find an injured wild animal, call a local vet or wildlife organisation for advice.

Top Tips

- Be sensible and cautious. Stay back and watch the animal for a while to see how badly injured it is. Wild animals can scratch and bite.
- Tell a grown-up, or call a vet or wildlife organisation for help.
- If you are helping a grown-up collect a wild animal, you can suggest that they line a well-ventilated cardboard box with newspaper or towels. Next, put on gloves, lift the animal (keeping it away from your face), and quickly put it into the box.
- There are some injured animals you should never try to handle: deer, seals, wild boar, otters, badgers, foxes, snakes, birds of prey (including owls), swans, geese, herons or gulls. Instead, call a vet or wildlife organisation.